READ That Label

Dear Reader

Labels on supermarket products are all designed to stand out. They are usually bright, colourful and attractive. Companies use labels like this so that we will buy their food and the many different kinds of products for sale.

There is usually another label on food products with information about what is inside the package.

IT'S IMPORTANT TO UNDERSTAND THOSE INFORMATION LABELS IF WE WANT TO CHOOSE HEALTHY FOODS.

This book will help you to learn more about these labels. This will make it easier for you to choose good products next time you're shopping.

John Parsons

NELSON
CENGAGE Learning™
For learning solutions, visit cengage.com.au

Contents

READ That Label

BAKED BEANS
good fibre for health
in natural tomato sauce

Read the Labels Before You Buy

Every time we shop in a supermarket, we have to make decisions. Each company wants us to buy their products. People need to know what they are buying before they can choose which product is the best. So read those labels first!

Get Informed

If we do not have accurate information about products, we could buy the wrong ones. We might choose a product that is:

- poor quality
- dangerous
- less nutritious
- stale or "off", or
- harmful to the environment.

Packaging Design

Manufacturers use packaging for many reasons. One reason is to design products that look attractive to catch our attention.

Shelf Location

In stores many items are located at eye-level on shelves. We can see those products more easily and we may buy those products first.

Persuasive Words

To persuade us to buy certain brands, stores place signs near products that sound good, such as:

A NEW, IMPROVED Computer Game!

FRESHER Fruit and Vegetables

New LONGER LASTING Batteries

A New BIODEGRADABLE Toilet Cleaner

More NATURAL Yoghurt

New RECYCLED Supermarket Bags!

But is something the best just because it:

- has the brightest packaging
- is a popular brand name, or
- uses persuasive words?

What we really need is reliable, factual information. Luckily, most countries have laws about what must appear on labels.

So take the time to read the labels!

2 Product Names

Read Carefully Before You Buy

When we are deciding what food or drinks to buy, we need to understand what product names mean on the packaging labels.

Labels on Products

It is important that we read packaging labels to check if the ingredients match the product names on the labels.

Tins of Spaghetti

Tins labelled "Spaghetti in Tomato Sauce" must only contain spaghetti in tomato sauce. They cannot contain any other foods.

100% Mince

A meat package labelled as "100% Mince" must only contain mince and no other ingredients. Read the use-by date on the label, too.

Sugar

Sugar used to sweeten products should come from sugar cane. Check the label for sugar content and any artificial sweeteners.

Read the Labels

You might think that reading labels is easy. But we still need to read the words carefully.

Does Banana-Flavoured Milk Contain Bananas?

Not always – it may only have banana-flavoured chemicals in the milk.

Are Flavours Natural?

Look carefully at the labels on foods or drinks that specify what kinds of flavours and ingredients were used to make it. It is important that we know the difference between natural and artificial flavours.

Does Orange Drink Contain Oranges?

No. Orange drink isn't the same thing as orange juice. It may contain only five per cent orange juice! Orange drink may also contain sugar, artificial flavour, colours and additives.

Ingredients on Labels

Pictures Help on Labels

A list of ingredients and their combined nutrition facts must appear on food packaging labels. Often, pictures of the ingredients are on labels, too. They help us to identify what is inside the packaging. Sometimes, a shorter list of ingredients may appear on the front of the packaging.

Which Fruit Salad Would You Choose?

Compare the labels on the two tins of fruit salad below. Which one would you choose to buy?

The label on this can provides some information about the fruit salad.

The label on this can provides more information about the fruit salad.

a machine-operated can-opener

The First Tin Cans

Today, many of our foods are preserved and sold in tin cans. In 1810, a Frenchman named Peter Durand invented the method for preserving foods in tin cans.

But people couldn't open them easily, so by the 1850s a tin-opener was invented. It is the can-opener designed in 1925 using two small wheels that we use to open cans today.

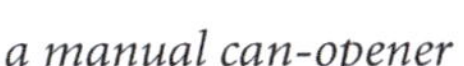

a manual can-opener

TIN CANS

A tin can is an airtight container used to store and transport goods. Tin cans are made of steel coated with a thin layer of tin. This is called "tin plate". Cans can also be made with aluminium or other metals.

4 Food Additives

Natural and **Artificial** Additives

Hundreds of additives can be added to foods. Many additives have several names, so numbers are used to identify them.

Here are some natural additives that you might see on food labels.

100 TURMERIC
(a natural orange or yellow colouring)

140 CHLOROPHYLL
(a natural green colouring)

406 AGAR
(a stabiliser)

302 CALCIUM
(for bone strength)

300 VITAMIN C
(an antioxidant)

Sometimes artificial additives are added to food or drink, too. Always read the labels first to know exactly what has been added to food. The chart opposite lists some artificial additives.

Additives	Purpose
Acids	These are preservatives. They help food last longer and make it taste fresher. A common food acid is vinegar.
Acidity Regulators	These can change the acidity of foods, give a sour taste to food and also help to preserve it.
Anti-Caking Agents	These stop powders such as flour or milk powder from clumping together.
Antioxidants	When food is exposed to oxygen it spoils many foods. Antioxidants slow down the rate that the food spoils.
Emulsifiers	These help oil and water to mix. They are used in products like mayonnaise and ice-cream.
Flavour Enhancers	These make a food's natural flavour seem stronger or more intense.
Food Colourings	These are added to food to make it look more attractive.
Humectants	These are added to food to stop it from drying out.
Preservatives	These preserve food. They stop or slow down the growth of microorganisms that make food go bad.
Stabilisers	These change the texture of food. Foods like bread, jam, jelly, ice-cream or yoghurt contain stabilisers.
Sweeteners	These make food taste sweeter.

Preservatives can prevent mould from growing on fresh foods.

A **Little** Bit of This, a **Little** Bit of That

We can compare the labels on different food packages to check which ones are higher in nutrients. Our bodies need plenty of water and a wide variety of nutritious foods to keep us healthy. It is important to have carbohydrates, fibre, protein and fats in our diets.

- Carbohydrates and fibre, about 50% of our daily food intake
- Protein, about 30% of our daily food intake
- Fats, about 20% of our daily food intake

This chart shows the percentage of carbohydrates, protein and fats we should aim to have each day.

Health

We All Need Some Fats

We all need to eat some fat to stay healthy. Some fats are healthier than others. Avocados, oily fish, olives and nuts contain healthy fat. Fatty meat, coconut cream and palm oil contain unhealthy fat.

Salmon contains healthy fats, oils and protein.

Recommended Daily Intake (RDI)

Some labels list RDIs. "RDI" stands for "Recommended Daily Intake". This is the amount of certain types of foods a person needs each day to stay healthy.

Some average RDIs for children aged 8 to 11 years are:

- fats or oils (margarine, oil) 50 grams
- carbohydrates (bread, rice, pasta) 225 grams
- fibre (vegetables, beans) 22 grams
- protein (meat, fish, chicken) 38 grams

RDIs depend on your age and gender. Boys and girls under the age of 13 usually need about three-quarters of an adult's RDI. People also have to be careful about the amount of salt, sugar and fat they eat in a day. By reading the nutritional facts on labels, people can be informed about how much of a certain food to eat.

A 100-gram avocado will give a person a high percentage of their RDI, as follows:

- fats and oils 15% of RDI
- carbohydrates 27% of RDI
- fibre 42% of RDI
- vitamin C 42% of RDI

avocados contain healthy fat and oil

6 Dates on Labels

Is it **Still Safe** to Eat?

Food can always become stale or spoilt, no matter how carefully we store or preserve it.

Bacteria and other microorganisms can get into fresh food and make it go "off". Bread can dry out, milk can go sour, cheese can grow mould, meat can go bad and fruit can turn rotten.

That's why most foods in supermarkets have dates on them. Dates help you to decide whether the food is fresh or safe to eat.

You can usually find two kinds of dates on food packaging – use-by dates and best-before dates.

a banana starting to rot

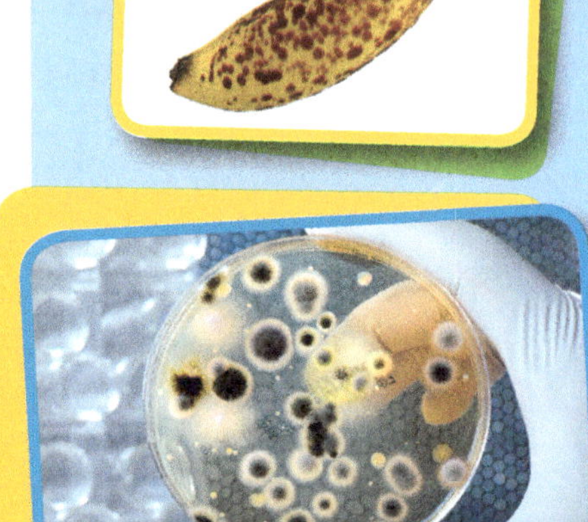

bacteria growing on a Petri dish in a laboratory

Health

How Do Bacteria Spoil Food?

There are many different kinds of bacteria that can spoil food, and sometimes it's enough to make you very sick. Some bacteria grow at low temperatures in the refrigerator. Others grow well at room temperature. The "danger zone" is between 4 degrees and 60 degrees Celsius. Some bacteria can double their numbers in as little as 20 minutes.

"That tastes awful!"

Most fresh milk has a use-by date on the carton.

Use-By Dates

Use-by dates are on many fresh foods, like yoghurt, milk, meat or baked goods. Use-by dates are usually found on foods that must be refrigerated. Food must be eaten before this date or it will start to spoil, or even make us ill.

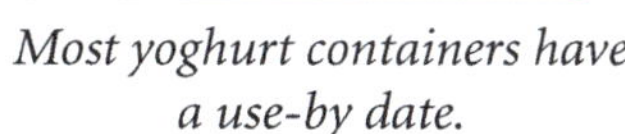

Most yoghurt containers have a use-by date.

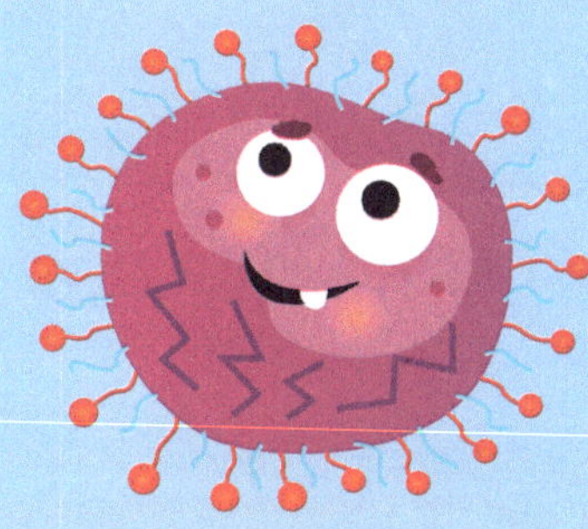

Best-Before Dates

Best-before dates are labelled on foods that can sit on shelves for a while. If a food is just past its best-before date, it can still usually be eaten safely. It might be a bit stale. It might not taste as good as it did when it was first made. But it shouldn't be bad or "off".

Egg cartons usually include a best-before date.

7 Food Storage

Be Careful with Food

We must store food properly to keep it safe to eat. Storage is important before and after we open a packet, jar, tin or sachet. Not storing food safely can lead to sickness, such as diarrhoea or vomiting. Here are two examples of food storage instructions found on labels.

"What's on that label?"

REFRIGERATE AFTER OPENING

This label may be on a bottle of orange juice.

STORE IN A COOL DRY PLACE

This label may be on a cereal packet.

Some labels also tell us how food should be treated after it is opened. Two examples are below.

CONSUME WITHIN THREE DAYS AFTER OPENING

This label may be on a jar of pasta sauce.

DO NOT REFREEZE

This label may be on a package of frozen fish.

"When did you first open the pasta jar?"

The First Electric Refrigerator

Many electric refrigerators were designed and invented in the 1880s. However, the first electric refrigerators manufactured in large numbers and suitable for use in homes became available in 1927. Separate freezers were first available for household use in the 1940s.

inside an electric refrigerator

Technology and History

Before Refrigerators

Before electric refrigerators, or before many people could afford to buy them, food was stored in iceboxes. Many iceboxes were built in the shape of a wooden hut. Its hollow walls were insulated to keep the temperature cool inside.

A large block of ice was placed on a tray in the top part of the ice box. A drip pan collected the melted ice underneath, and the water was emptied out of the pan daily.

More ice was bought from "icemen", who delivered large iceblocks on wagons, carts or trucks.

an icebox

8 Egg Carton Labels

Read the Label and Choose

ORGANIC

One of the most popular and nutritious foods are eggs. Often, people want to buy eggs from farms where the hens have been allowed to live freely and not in cages. More and more people care about:

- where the hens live
- what the hens eat
- how the hens are treated.

free-range hens

caged hens

Egg Carton Labels

People read the labels on egg cartons to help them choose which eggs to buy. Here are two examples of egg cartons.

Read egg carton labels to check if the hens are well cared for.

Eggs are best stored in their cartons and kept in the fridge.

Persuasive Labels

Many hen farmers want to feed and care for their hens in special ways. When they do, they will add short labels to the egg cartons to catch people's attention.

ORGANIC — *This means that the hens have been fed organic food. These eggs should be higher in nutrients than non-organic eggs.*

BIODYNAMIC — *This means that the hens eat grass grown in rich, natural soil, free of artificial pesticides.*

HORMONE FREE — *Be careful if you see this label on an egg carton. Usually all eggs are hormone free anyway.*

Health

Why Eat Eggs?

Eggs are a good source of protein.
One serve of eggs can provide children with high amounts of protein. It provides:

- girls aged 9–13 with 36% of their daily protein needs
- boys aged 9–13 with 32% of their daily protein needs.

There are also healthy fats, antioxidants and ten different vitamins and minerals in eggs.

Eggs can be sold on large trays.

Labels Front and Back

Baked Beans for Breakfast

If you ate a quarter of a cup of baked beans for breakfast, here is an example of their nutritional value:

- carbohydrates = 14 grams
- protein = 5 grams
- dietary fibre = 6 grams
- fat = 0.5 grams.

Baked beans are a popular and nutritious food.

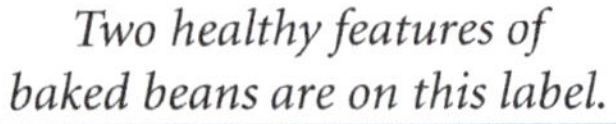
Two healthy features of baked beans are on this label.

BAKED BEANS

Baked beans are beans cooked in a sauce. Most canned baked beans are made from navy beans, which are small and white.

LABEL 1

AMOUNT Per Serve	1 cup
Kilojoules	1205.4 kilojoules
Total Fat	5 g
Cholesterol	2.24 mg
Salt	60 mg
Potassium	22 mg
Total Carbohydrates	39.86 g
Dietary Fibre	31.56 g
Sugar	2.5 g
Protein	10.4 g
Vitamin A	195.02 IU
Vitamin C	2.88 mg
Calcium	211.90 mg
Iron	8.23 mg

Note: IU is a measurement used for some vitamins.

LABEL 2

AMOUNT Per Serve	1 cup
Kilojoules	1545.6 kilojoules
Total Fat	17.02 g
Cholesterol	15.54 mg
Salt	1113.7 mg
Potassium	608.65 mg
Total Carbohydrates	59.86 g
Dietary Fibre	17.87 g
Sugar	16.91 g
Protein	17.48 g
Vitamin A	225.33 IU
Vitamin C	5.96 mg
Calcium	124.32 mg
Iron	4.48 mg

Label Questions

Which label tells you that the food has:

- less fat?
- more protein?
- more carbohydrates?
- more fibre?
- less sugar?
- less salt?

Environment Feature

Landfill

Waste: Reduce and Recycle

Every person produces about two tonnes of waste each year. This means millions of tonnes of waste are buried as landfill. We throw away more waste each year. About a quarter of that waste is packaging from food and other goods.

Why Is Waste Harmful?

Throwing away this much waste harms the environment. When waste rots it produces methane gas, which can cause explosions. It is also a dangerous greenhouse gas. Chemicals, heavy metals and bacteria from landfill sites leak into the surrounding earth and water underground.

Some modern landfill sites try to reduce some of this damage by converting the gas emissions into energy at power stations.

a landfill site

bulldozing landfill

Reduce Waste

Here are some simple ideas to help reduce waste:

- reduce product packaging
- produce packaging out of materials that can decay easily
- produce packages and containers that can be refilled, recycled or reused
- produce packages out of recycled materials.

Why Should I Recycle?

The best solution is not to make packaging in the first place. But this is difficult. The second-best solution is to reuse products and to reduce the amount of waste being produced. People and businesses can save money and help the environment by recycling and reducing waste.

"My job is to put the cans in the recycling bin."

"Mum and I have cleaned all the bottles before putting them into the recycling bin."

Less Energy to Recycle?

Recycling something may use less energy than producing it from raw materials. It may also create less pollution. For example, it takes a lot of electricity to produce aluminium from bauxite, but very little to recycle it. Always rinse out your aluminium cans before recycling.

This recycle symbol often appears on labels to encourage people to recycle.

"Our job is to put all the paper into the recycling bin."

Index

Glossary

aluminium	A lightweight metal that does not rust
bauxite	The raw natural mineral that contains aluminium
biodegradable	Able to naturally decay, break down or rot
cholesterol	A type of fat that can affect the health of people's hearts and arteries
microorganisms	Living things that are so small they cannot be seen without the aid of a microscope
nutrients	The substances in foods that all living things need to stay fit and healthy
organic	Foods that are grown or produced without the use of chemicals, such as pesticides
pesticide	A chemical that is used to kill or keep pests, such as insects, away from growing crops